Ever since I was little, my biggest dream was to have a sibling. Sometimes it felt like I never would, but I trusted that God had a plan—and he did! After years and years of praying, I got the perfect Christmas gift. My little sister, Dolly, is the best thing that has ever happened to me. She's funny, cute, happy, thoughtful, sweet, and considerate, and she never lets anyone frown. She's my light, and I love her more than life.

Daisy

To our precious Daisy, who longed for, prayed for,
and never stopped believing in her dream

ABOUT THIS BOOK: The illustrations for this book were done in Photoshop. This book was edited by Deirdre Jones and designed by Sheila Smallwood and Saho Fujii. The production was supervised by Nyamekye Waliyaya, and the production editor was Marisa Finkelstein. The text was set in Cochin, and the display type was hand-lettered by David Coulson.

Copyright © 2020 by Kimberly Schlapman • Illustrations by Morgan Huff • Hand lettering by David Coulson • Cover illustration by Morgan Huff • Cover design by Sheila Smallwood and Saho Fujii • Cover copyright © 2020 by Hachette Book Group, Inc. • Hachette Book Group supports the right to free expression and the value of copyright. The purpose of copyright is to encourage writers and artists to produce the creative works that enrich our culture. • The scanning, uploading, and distribution of this book without permission is a theft of the author's intellectual property. If you would like permission to use material from the book (other than for review purposes), please contact permissions@hbgusa.com. Thank you for your support of the author's rights. • Little, Brown and Company • Hachette Book Group • 1290 Avenue of the Americas, New York, NY 10104 • Visit us at LBYR.com • First Edition: October 2020 • Little, Brown and Company is a division of Hachette Book Group, Inc. • The Little, Brown name and logo are trademarks of Hachette Book Group, Inc. • The publisher is not responsible for websites (or their content) that are not owned by the publisher. • Library of Congress Cataloging-in-Publication Data • Names: Schlapman, Kimberly, author. | Huff, Morgan, illustrator. • Title: A dolly for Christmas : the true story of a family's Christmas miracle / by Kimberly Schlapman; illustrated by Morgan Huff. • Description: First edition. | New York, NY : Little, Brown and Company, 2020. | Audience: Ages 4-8. | Summary: "A young girl's Christmas wish for a baby sibling is granted in this heartwarming adoption story" —Provided by publisher. • Identifiers: LCCN 2020018831 | ISBN 9780316542968 (hardcover) | ISBN 9780316542999 (ebook) | ISBN 9780316542975 (ebook other) • Subjects: CYAC. Only child—Fiction. | Family life—Fiction. | Adoption—Fiction. | Christmas—Fiction. • Classification: LCC PZ7.1.S336155 Dol 2020 | DDC [E]—dc23 • LC record available at https://lccn.loc.gov/2020018831 • ISBNs: 978-0-316-54296-8 (hardcover), 978-0-316-54300-2 (ebook), 978-0-316-54299-9 (ebook), 978-0-316-54298-2 (ebook) • PRINTED IN THE UNITED STATES OF AMERICA • PHX •
10 9 8 7 6 5 4 3 2 1

LITTLE BIG TOWN'S

KIMBERLY SCHLAPMAN

A Dolly for Christmas

THE TRUE STORY OF A
FAMILY'S CHRISTMAS MIRACLE

ILLUSTRATED BY MORGAN HUFF

LITTLE, BROWN AND COMPANY
New York Boston

Christmas is a time for wishes and miracles.

Daisy's family had a wish.

And they needed a miracle.

Daisy's parents had been trying for a long,
long time to have a baby. But it wasn't working.

"Mommy, if I never have a brother or sister, *my* children will never have aunts or uncles or cousins."

"Keep wishing, Daisy Pearl," her mother said. "And keep praying for a miracle."

So Daisy wished every day.

When she woke up in the morning.

While she played with her friends.

Before she had supper.

And every night before bed.

No matter how much she wished,
though, a baby didn't come.

Daisy felt frustrated, and her parents seemed so sad. Wishing and praying weren't *doing* anything. It was time to take action.

When no one was watching, Daisy wrote a letter…

...and slipped it into a special mailbox.

Dear Santa,

Really, all I want for christmas is a baby Brother or sister.

love,
Daisy

And a few days later, just to be sure,
Daisy talked to Santa in person, too.

"Thank you for trying to help our family, Daisy," said her mother.

"But sometimes…we have to wait for our prayers to be answered, no matter how much we want something," said her father. "God will give us the perfect gift when the time is right."

Daisy thought about *waiting* the rest of the night.
During the car ride home.

As she ate her supper.

While she played with her friends.

And before she went to bed.

I wonder if a little brother or sister is waiting for me, too, she thought as she drifted off to sleep.
Don't worry, Baby. I'll pray for you as long as it takes.

Daisy!

Daisy!

It's our baby!
It's our baby!

Ten days later, after so many years of wishing
and hoping and praying and waiting…
Daisy's family got their miracle.

A *Dolly* for Christmas.

A Note from Kimberly Schlapman

As far back as I can remember, my greatest dream was to be a mommy. When my first husband passed away suddenly, not only did I lose my companion but what I thought was my chance at being a mother. I later remarried an incredible man who taught me to love again, and we were blessed with a joyful, high-spirited baby girl named Daisy. Only years later, when my husband and I tried to have another child, would we find out that Daisy was a miracle and becoming pregnant with a second baby would be difficult.

From the time Daisy was very small, she badly wanted a sibling. Every night she asked God for a baby. My husband and I tried *all* measures to make that happen, but each ended in loss, heartbreak, and disappointment. We finally decided to start the adoption process, and Daisy—still positive and hopeful about a sibling—continued to pray. One Christmas she even asked Santa Claus for a baby! *A Dolly for Christmas* is the true story of a little girl who finally had her prayers answered in the most spectacular way: Right at Christmastime, our second daughter, Dolly Grace, arrived. Now my girls are inseparable, and their relationship is magical; it's true love!

I decided to share the story of Daisy's wish and Dolly's homecoming to encourage anyone struggling with infertility issues or with the arduous adoption process to stay hopeful and to believe in miracles. Christmas wishes hold a special kind of magic, and while waiting is so hard, the gift of a child and of a family becoming whole make it more than worth it.

Kimberly Schlepman

Dolly at two months old.

Jessie Roesch

Best friends Dolly and Daisy.

Rachael Black

Our family, whole and happy.